ALAN FREDMAN

To. Kenneth
Love, Carolynn & Wayne
Aug 4.19

ISBN 0 86163 117 X

Printed in Belgium

BEDTIME TALES

Written by Hayden McAllister

AWARD PUBLICATIONS – LONDON

Rabbits Can't Fly!

Tilly the Rabbit was bobbing along when she heard a bluebird singing.

"It's a beautiful morning and singing makes me happy!" chirped the little bird.

Tilly the Rabbit hopped along a bit further until she came to the little pool where the Green Frog lived.

"Hello Green Frog!" greeted Tilly. "You look happy!"

"I am happy!" said the Green Frog. "I've been sitting croaking on my favourite stone all morning!"

Tilly walked on a little way. "I wonder what it's like to fly like Bluebird?" mused Tilly. "And I wonder what it's like to swim like Green Frog?"

So Tilly decided – just this once – to try and fly like Bluebird. She went home and picked up her umbrella. Then she climbed a tree near the Green Frog's pool and with the umbrella open like a parachute, Tilly jumped off a branch.

"But rabbits can't fly!" squawked Bluebird.

"You're right!" groaned Tilly as she fell – SPLASH – into the pond. "And they can't swim very well either," croaked the Green Frog.

"In future I'll stick to being a rabbit," spluttered Tilly Rabbit. "After all it's what makes *me* happy!"

Summer Dreams

When Felicity Fieldmouse awoke one bright July morning, she just *knew* it was going to be a warm sunny day.

After eating a peanut for breakfast Felicity strolled outside into the early morning sunshine. She could feel the warm earth under her tiny feet. The grass had a lovely fragrance and the breeze was gentle.

Felicity walked on, past a mushroom and a toadstool, and finally stopped in her favourite place amongst the flowers.

There was *nothing* Felicity liked better than to lie down on a warm summer's day and listen to the rustle of the daisies and the faint tinkling of the bell flowers.

It was the kind of day Felicity had dreamed about all winter. . . . And here it was at last!

Being Together

Kitty the Kitten and Mandy the Mouse were very special friends. When Mandy Mouse wanted to go shopping to buy herself some cheese and biscuits, Kitty the Kitten would go along with her to the supermarket.

And when Kitty the Kitten wanted to go to the fishmongers to buy herself some fish, Mandy Mouse would keep her company. Mandy and Kitty liked to be together *wherever* they went.

On the morning of Kitty's birthday, Mandy turned up with a present: "It's a flower from the fields where we play," said Mandy.

"It's lovely!" exclaimed Kitty. "I'll put it in a vase filled with water."

Posting Letters

Toby Bear was a postman. Every morning Toby would say 'goodbye' to Tweet his pet bird and plod down to the post office.

At the post office Toby Bear would collect all the letters that needed delivering. Then he would set off on his round.

One morning, just as Toby was about to say 'goodbye' to Tweet, Tweet chirped: "Why not take me with you, Toby?"

"That's a good idea," said Toby. "I could do with some company."

Tweet was a clever little bird and soon he was picking up letters in his beak and posting them through people's letter boxes.

"I'll get you a proper job at the post office if you like," said Toby.

"Yes!" chirped Tweet. "I can post all the *air* mail letters."

Playing Marbles

Sam and Stewart were playing marbles in a quiet little corner of the park.

At first it was only the two boys playing there in the shade of a huge tree.

There was a nice smooth piece of ground beneath the tree and Sam and Stewart felt it was the perfect place for a game of marbles.

"Click, click," went the marbles. "Good shot!" said Stewart.

A little kitten called Toodles thought it was an interesting game and came to watch.

Two little girls wandering by, came over to see what the boys were doing.

"I don't know what this game is called," whispered one little girl.

"Marbles," said Sam. "They call it marbles. But girls don't often play."

A blue tit flew down to a lower branch of the tree to see what was going on. Then a squirrel joined the audience.

"I wonder if this game could be played with acorns?" thought the squirrel.

Screecher the Monkey

Screecher the Monkey wanted to sing nearly all the time. The trouble was – Screecher the Monkey couldn't sing very well. In fact, his singing was so bad that the jungle animals would hide or cover their ears if they saw Screecher coming.

One wise old elephant even stuck coconuts in his ears so he couldn't hear a note Screecher sang.

Screecher had two pals called Monty and Maurice and they would all play in the jungle together, swinging in the trees and eating bananas.

If Screecher wanted to start singing when he was with Monty and Maurice, they'd tell him to climb into a tree and sing by himself.

When Screecher was singing high in a tree, Monty and Maurice couldn't hear him. And usually Screecher's awful voice would make some of the leaves and bananas fall off the trees. With the leaves Monty and Maurice would make a nice warm bed for themselves. And, of course, they'd eat the bananas!

On the River

When Aunty Rita Rabbit woke up and looked out of her bedroom window she was pleased to see the sun shining. Aunty Rita lived in a small white cottage near the river and, although she liked to look at the river, she was a little frightened of water.

But today her nephew Roger Rabbit was coming to see her. And he'd promised to take her out on the river in a boat. Just fancy! Actually floating on the water like a duck!

When Roger Rabbit arrived he was wearing his smart new hat. "I don't often wear hats," he said, "but it will keep the sun off my head."

"Then I'll take my sun brolly," said Aunty Rita. "Just in case it gets too hot."

In the afternoon after dinner, Roger took his Aunty Rita out boating. It was like a dream come true for Aunty Rita as she watched the river bank drift by. They passed flowers and duck and fish and Aunty Rita had a lovely time!

Jimbo and Pedro

Jimbo the Elephant was bored. So he went to see his friend Pedro the Panda. "Oh dear. I'm so terribly bored!" he said to Pedro.

"Bored?" How can you possibly be bored?" asked Pedro the Panda. "I'm always so busy *doing* things."

"What kind of things?" yawned Jimbo the Elephant.

"Watching the stars. Reading story books. Eating sandwiches. Playing on the banana slide."

"Banana slide!" cried Jimbo, pricking up his ears. "That sounds like fun!"

"It is fun!" laughed Pedro. "Why not come along to the banana slide now?"

So Pedro and Jimbo played on the banana slide for hours. Jimbo enjoyed himself so much he wondered how he could *ever* have been bored!

Joe the Clown

Joe was a housepainter. In his wheelbarrow he carried pots of paint and brushes. Across the top of his barrow he carried his stepladders.

Sometimes he would fall off his ladder and land on his head and other times he would put his foot in a pot of paint.

Joe began to think about that. He thought: "If I put my foot in a pot of paint, people think I'm a bad housepainter. But if I were a clown, they'd think I was a *good* clown."

So Joe became a clown. And a very good clown too!

The Yellow Spectacles

Arnold the Alligator was swimming along in the river – when suddenly he felt like having a chat with a friend.

"I'll go and talk to my friend Archie," he said to himself.

After Arnold Alligator had paddled a few yards, he saw a shape which looked like Archie the Alligator floating in the water ahead.

"Hello Archie," said Arnold. "Miserable weather we're having?"

Archie didn't say anything.

"He must be asleep," thought Arnold. "I'll have to speak up. Hello Archie!" he cried.

Archie still didn't say anything.

Then Arnold realised he'd mistaken a floating tree trunk for his friend Archie.

"I'll have to go and get myself some spectacles," muttered Arnold. "Green ones? No. I'd probably lose them in the grass. I know, I'll get myself a pair of *yellow* spectacles."

Delia the Dove

Delia the Dove always liked flowers. A long time ago when she was a baby bird and couldn't fly, she fell out of her nest and landed on a soft bed of marigolds. Those marigolds saved her life.

Mr Jones liked marigolds too. He had a window box at every window of his big white house, full of brightly coloured flowers.

Mr Jones also liked doves. One day Mr Jones met Delia the Dove as he was planting out some flowers in a window box. She came and landed on the edge of the window box with a sprig of heather in her beak.

Mr Jones planted the heather in his garden, and it grew.

Every day after that Mr Jones would leave some peanuts in the corner of his window box for Delia the Dove.

Sometimes the children would wait at the other side of the window and watch her eat.

"Coo, coo, coo!" Delia would say, before flying away. "Thank–you!"

High Flying Kite

Sally had been given a new kite by her Uncle Fred. She was very excited and straight after dinner she went to fly her kite in the park. It was a nice breezy day and kites of all shapes and colours were flying in the sky. But poor Sally couldn't get *her* kite to fly.

Her friend Johnny came along and he tried to help. But Sally's kite just wouldn't fly.

Suddenly Johnny had an idea! There was a man in the fields near the park who had a gas balloon. So Johnny asked the man if Sally could go up in the balloon and fly her kite from the balloon basket.

The man agreed and Sally climbed into the balloon with her kite.

Once in the air, Sally's little kite flew perfectly. "It's obviously a high flying kite," she said to herself.

Marcus the Mouse

Marcus the Mouse was sniffing in the grass and whistling to himself.

"Ah! What a perfectly splendid day!" he squeaked. "If I were a composer I'd write a song about such a perfectly splendid day –"

WHOOSH! Marcus the Mouse was nearly squashed flat as a great, big dog went hurtling by.

"Good gracious!" squeaked Marcus. "That must be Bingo the Dog, escaped from his owner again. He's obviously chasing a cat."

"Now what I can't understand," mused Marcus, "is why human beings don't take mice out for a walk with a lead and a collar.

We wouldn't take up as much room. We wouldn't cost as much to feed . . ."

"And what's more," added Marcus the Mouse. "We wouldn't go chasing after cats."

The Kangaroo Car

Fred and Mabel Fox had sold their bicycles and bought themselves a brand new sports car. It was called a kangaroo car.

"Why is it called a kangaroo car?" asked Mabel.

"I don't know," answered Fred. "But kangaroos move along at great speed. And that's just what we want to do in our new kangaroo car!"

So Fred and Mabel climbed into their new car and went for a drive into the country.

At first Fred drove the kangaroo car very carefully. When they turned left, Mabel put out her hand to signal 'left'. And when they turned right, Fred put out his right hand to signal 'right'.

When at last they came to a long stretch of road Fred decided to go faster. But the moment the car went faster it began to bounce along.

"Oh no! This is terrible!" cried Fred. "The car is *bouncing* along like a kangaroo."

"I think I prefer my bicycle!" gasped Mabel.

Charlie and Nipper

Charlie the Cat had been trying to catch Nipper the Mouse for years. Charlie was a *real* cat, and the one thing he didn't like was a clever little mouse like Nipper.

While Charlie was waiting outside Nipper's hole, Nipper the Mouse was painting a picture – of *himself*! When he'd finished it looked just like him! "Now there are two Nippers!" he chuckled.

"I'll stick this picture just inside my mouse hole," he squeaked to himself. "And while Charlie is keeping an eye on my picture – I'll nip out the back door and go and buy a cheese yoghurt."

When Nipper came back later, Charlie was still there, watching the picture.

"He'd make a good watch dog!" chuckled Nipper.

Little Lamb

Little Lamb went skipping through the grass.

"The grass is so green and the ground is so full of bounce – just like me!" he thought to himself.

As he tripped along, Little Lamb saw a bright green hill.

"In a hop and a skip and a jump, I'll be at the top of that hill," he said to himself.

And so with a hop and a skip and a jump, Little Lamb found himself on top of the hill. There he found some juicy green grass and beautiful flowers.

"This looks the perfect place to bring my brothers and sisters," smiled Little Lamb.

Short Sighted Rabbit

One day Professor Rabbit (who wore spectacles) was walking through the wood deep in thought. "One and one make two," he muttered to himself. He was so busy muttering to himself, he nearly bumped into a green grass snake.

"Hello!" said the green grass snake. "You're the first rabbit I've ever seen wearing glasses."

Professor Rabbit stopped. "Pardon? Did you say something?"

"You're the first rabbit I've seen wearing glasses," repeated the grass snake.

"And you're the first grass snake I've seen wearing a bow tie," said Professor Rabbit.

"What is a bow tie?" asked the grass snake.

"It's that red bow shaped object on your neck of course," said the rabbit.

"It's not a bow tie," said the grass snake. "It's my friend Herbert, the red butterfly. He's just drying his wings."

"I think I need a new pair of glasses!" said Professor Rabbit.

The Silver Ball

It was Christmas time and Skip the Mouse could hear everyone enjoying themselves from his mousehole in the skirting board.

"I do hope they've left a Christmas present for me," he squeaked. "Even if it's only cheese wrapped in tinsel."

In the afternoon when everyone was out, Skip played at the foot of the Christmas tree. There, he found a silver ball which had fallen from the Christmas tree. When Skip looked at his reflection in the silver ball it made him laugh.

"There's a funny faced mouse in there!" he chuckled. "And whenever I laugh, he laughs too! I wonder if he's got any cheese?"

The Clockwork Carrot

Tufty the Rabbit had been given lots of presents at Christmas; a pair of rabbit socks from Aunty Bunny, a rabbit handkerchief from Great Aunt Bunny and a rabbit tie from Grandma Bunny.

Tufty opened another present and found a nice red carrot inside. But when Tufty put the carrot on the floor, the carrot began to jump and wriggle across the room!

"It's alive!" gasped Tufty.

Later Tufty realised that it was a *clockwork* carrot!

"I'll take it to rabbit school with me," he said. "And I'll show it to all my friends!"

The Two Hippo's

The two hippopotamuses (hippos for short) lumbered down a country lane. It was a hot day. In fact it was a *very* hot day, especially for hippos who like the cool of the river mud. "Phew!" said one. "It's hot!"

"Phew! You're telling me!" said the other.

"Phew!" said one. "I'd like a nice cool plod in a nice cool river."

"Phew! You're telling me!" said the other.

"Phew!" said one, wiping his big forehead. "I'd like a nice crater full of ice-cubes and fresh oozy mud to slowly sink into . . ."

"Phew! You're telling me!" said the other.

"Why do you keep saying Phew – you're telling me?" asked one.

"Because it's Phew! Too hot to argue," said the other.

"Phew! You're telling me!" said the first one.